THE ONE-EYED GIANT
— AND —
OTHER MONSTERS
FROM THE GREEK MYTHS

· BY ANNE ROCKWELL ·

GREENWILLOW BOOKS, NEW YORK

AUTHOR'S NOTE

All the monsters in this book are fantasy creatures. Everywhere in the world people have imagined monsters, made up stories about them, and tried, in art, to show us what they looked like. The stories in this book were told centuries ago by the people of ancient Greece.

No one knows why people have always enjoyed inventing monsters and making up stories about them. Perhaps it is because these imagined monsters are not quite as frightening as some things we fear that have no name.

There are different kinds of monsters, and they come in all sizes. Some are part human, part beast. Some are creatures so ugly no one can look at them.

Heroes and heroines are people like you and me, but they are braver, smarter, and stronger than we are. In stories heroes often destroy the monsters who threaten them.

I have always enjoyed reading about monsters and imagining what they looked like. These Greek myths are among my favorites. I hope you will enjoy reading them and perhaps invent some monster stories of your own. They are for all children to enjoy, especially my own grandchildren— Nicholas, Julianna, Nigel, and Christian.

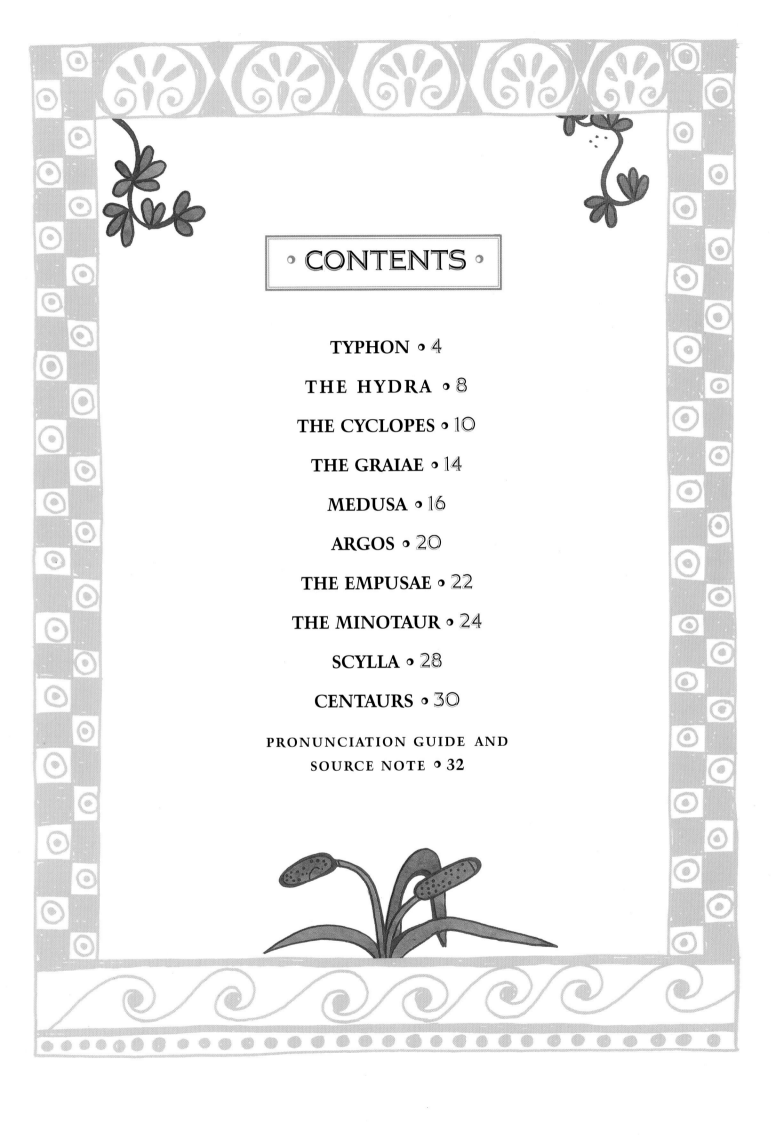

· CONTENTS ·

TYPHON

Of all the monsters that ever were, Typhon was the biggest. His head, which nearly touched the stars, was that of an enormous mule. He could imitate the sound of any beast. The spread of his wings darkened the earth. His arms stretched farther than the eye can see, and his hundreds of fingers were the heads of serpents. Where his legs should have been were great coiled serpents. Fire and burning rocks poured out of his mouth whenever he roared. He was married to the terrible snake-woman, Echidna, who ate men raw. The two of them were the proud parents of a hundred terrible monsters.

Typhon was afraid of no one, not even the gods. One day he decided to go to war with the immortal ones who lived on Mount Olympus. The gods and goddesses were so terrified at the sight of him that they all ran away and disguised themselves as animals. But Typhon pursued them until he finally captured almighty Zeus himself and imprisoned him in a cave. Here the ruler of the gods

remained until his messenger, crafty Hermes, finally set him free.

Zeus regained his courage. He hurled thunderbolts at Typhon until one wounded the monster. Then Zeus picked up a mountain and threw it at him with all his godly force.

Typhon roared out in pain. Zeus had finally won. The mountain was even larger than Typhon. It covered every bit of him.

The gods and goddesses returned home in peace, but Typhon continued to bellow from beneath the mountain until fire and rocks from his mouth spurted up and made a volcano called Etna.

THE HYDRA

One particularly horrible child of Typhon and Echidna was the Hydra, a huge monster with many serpent heads. He lived in a swamp, where his venom poisoned the water all around. No one could kill him, for whenever anyone chopped off one of his heads, another immediately grew in its place.

Heracles, a powerful hero and the strongest mortal who ever lived, decided to do battle with the monster. The Hydra summoned his friend, a gigantic crab, to help him fight Heracles. But Heracles, too, had brought a helper named Iolaus.

As fast as Heracles cut off one of the Hydra's heads, Iolaus seared the stump with his red-hot sword, so it could never grow back. At last all the Hydra's heads were gone. And Heracles tossed the giant crab out of the swamp, high up into the sky, where we can see it still as the constellation known as Cancer.

THE CYCLOPES

The Cyclopes were giants. Each had only one enormous eye in the middle of his forehead. They lived in wild, faraway places where there were no laws. Each Cyclops lived alone, tending his sheep and goats. One was named Polyphemus, and he was the son of Poseidon, god of the sea.

Long ago a man named Odysseus was sailing home from war. He and his crew went ashore on Polyphemus' island, where they made themselves comfortable in the giant's cave.

When Polyphemus returned that evening with his flocks, he was furious to see strangers in his home. He closed the entrance to the cave with a gigantic rock only he was strong enough to move. Then he killed and ate some of the unlucky sailors.

Odysseus didn't try to take revenge that night, but while Polyphemus slept, he stayed awake, waiting. When he heard the giant snoring loudly, he poked a red-hot stick into

his one enormous eye and blinded him.

In the morning Odysseus and his remaining crew clung to the woolly bellies of the giant's rams. The animals left the cave as Polyphemus counted them one by one by patting their backs. The blinded Polyphemus couldn't see that Odysseus and the sailors were safely hidden beneath his long-haired beasts.

Odysseus paid a high price for his cleverness. He hadn't known that Polyphemus was the son of Poseidon, and now the god of the sea was angry with him. He punished Odysseus by making it impossible for him to return to his home on the small, rocky island of Ithaca.

But although clever and crafty Odysseus had made an enemy of the powerful god, he was also beloved by the goddess Athene. After many years she helped the wanderer return home, where he could tell of his adventure in the cave of Polyphemus.

THE GRAIAE

There were once three sisters: Pemphredo, Enyo, and Deino. They were called the Graiae because of the long, stringy gray hair they had been born with. They had only one eye and one tooth to share among the three of them, so they always stayed together.

One day a hero named Perseus stole their one eye and their one tooth. He swore he wouldn't give back either eye or tooth until they told him where he could find their other sister, the dreadful Gorgon Medusa.

At last Pemphredo, Enyo, and Deino agreed to reveal Medusa's hiding place. They also told Perseus where to find the winged sandals and helmet he would need for his journey.

Perseus returned their eye and tooth and quickly left in search of Medusa.

MEDUSA

Medusa, the sister of the Graiae, was a monster called a Gorgon. She had the body of a normal woman, but a hideous face. She had huge, sharp teeth, two of which curved outward like the tusks of a wild boar. Her tongue always stuck out, and her eyes glowed like fire. Her hair was made of poisonous snakes that coiled and twisted, hissing and spitting. She was so terrifying that anyone who looked at her was instantly turned to stone.

Perseus, wearing the winged sandals and helmet Medusa's sisters, the Graiae, had helped him obtain, flew to where she lived. He took with him a silver shield that shone like a mirror and a sharp sickle. When he arrived at a lonely field crowded with stones that had the shapes of human beings, he knew he had come to the right place. The stones were all that was left of people who had dared look at the Gorgon Medusa.

Perseus was clever. He never looked directly at Medusa. Instead he only viewed her image reflected in his shining shield. Gazing carefully at her reflection, he used his sickle

to cut off her head. As Medusa died, a beautiful winged horse named Pegasus sprang from her body.

Perseus kept his eyes closed tight while he put the monster's horrible head into a leather bag. Then he mounted the flying horse and rode away. He brought the leather bag, with all the snakes still hissing inside, to the goddess Athene. From that day on Athene wore it on her golden armor to frighten off her enemies.

Unfortunately, as Perseus rode through the sky, a few drops of Medusa's blood dripped out of the bag onto the desert sands below. Each drop became a field of poisonous serpents, and no one ever went to that desert again.

No one.

ARGOS

Argos was as large and strong as a bull. He had a hundred eyes and could see everywhere. No secret could be kept from him.

The goddess Hera loved this monster like a son. The truth is, he was not an altogether bad monster. It was Argos who had killed the horrible Echidna, wife of Typhon. Nevertheless, both gods and mortals hated him for his spying eyes that could see everything they were doing. Yet no harm ever came to him, for the powerful Hera protected him and no mortal could ever destroy him.

Hera's husband, the great Zeus, had the habit of falling in love with other women, which made his wife jealous. One of the women Zeus loved was a young girl named Io. Hera was so jealous of the beautiful girl that she turned her into a snow-white cow. She sent Argos to watch over Io and keep her away from Zeus.

This infuriated the ruler of the gods. He sent his messenger, the god Hermes, to kill Argos. Hermes did so, but Hera brought her beloved Argos back to life again as a peacock. Then she placed his many glowing eyes in the bird's long tail.

THE EMPUSAE

The Empusae were the three repulsive daughters of Hecate, the witch goddess. Their only companions were the dead, and they themselves looked like ghosts. They were also very dirty and stank horribly.

Whenever dogs howled late on moonless nights, it meant the Empusae were roaming about. These monsters liked to hide near dark and lonely crossroads, where they moaned and wailed to frighten nighttime travelers. Those who journeyed frequently along such roads knew they could chase the dreaded spooks away simply by insulting them and calling them names, but most travelers didn't know that.

In order to bribe the Empusae to stay away from crossroads, people often left plates of rotten fish and the flesh of dogs. It was disgusting food, but the Empusae loved such treats. And after they had eaten, they usually behaved themselves—until they were hungry again.

THE MINOTAUR

Long ago, in the land of Crete, a queen gave birth to a child with the body of a baby boy and the head of a bull calf. Hideous as he was, the queen loved him.

The baby grew up to be a monster who lived on nothing but human flesh. He was called the Minotaur. This royal monster was so dangerous that the king and queen hired an architect named Daedalus to build a twisting maze inside the palace walls. The Minotaur's room was deep in the maze so that he could never escape, but neither could his victims.

Across the sea was the city of Athens. The people of Athens and Crete were enemies. To keep peace, the king and queen of Crete demanded that every year seven boys and seven girls from Athens be sent across the sea to be fed to the Minotaur.

One year a young prince named Theseus was among the Athenians picked to be sacrificed. But Theseus was not planning to die. Instead he plotted to kill the Minotaur.

The king and queen had a daughter, Princess Ariadne, who fell in love with the handsome victim. She secretly offered to help Theseus kill the monster, on condition that Theseus marry her. He agreed, so Ariadne gave him a ball of fine silk thread and a sharp sword and told him what to do.

As he entered the maze, Theseus trailed the thread behind him until he reached the place where the monster lay sleeping. He grabbed the Minotaur by the hair and killed him. Then Theseus escaped by following the thread, which led him out again.

He and his companions boarded their ship, taking Ariadne with them. But on the way home they stopped at the island of Naxos, and everyone went ashore. The Cretan princess lay down on the beach and went to sleep. Theseus left her there and returned home, a great hero.

It happened that the god Dionysus soon discovered the abandoned princess and wakened her. Ariadne remained on Naxos to worship Dionysus from that day on.

SCYLLA

Scylla lived in a cave on a huge rock that rose from the sea. Her home was near a whirlpool called Charybdis that sucked ships down into the water, and close to a small island where the Sirens lived. Sirens were monsters with the bodies of birds and the heads of women who sang enchanting songs to lure ships and sailors to either the cave of Scylla or the whirlpool of Charybdis.

Scylla had six heads. Each head had three rows of sharp teeth. She wore a skirt woven of dog's heads. She had twelve feet to help her climb to the highest point on her island, so she could spot ships far out at sea. The flesh of sailors was her favorite treat. If any ship drifted near her rock, she would capture the crew and eat the sailors, six at a time. She could never be killed.

No one knows where Scylla came from. Some say she was one of the many children of Typhon and Echidna, but others insist she was once a beautiful maiden who fell in love with a merman whom the enchantress Circe also loved. Circe was jealous of Scylla and cast a spell over her, making her so hideous no one would ever love her again.

It worked. No one ever did.

CENTAURS

Centaurs had the bodies of horses, but the heads and shoulders of men. It was said that a cloud gave birth to them. They lived far away from civilization in forests of oak, high in the mountains. Centaurs were brutal and greedy. Humans avoided them, and here is the reason why.

Long ago a group of people called Lapiths were arranging a great wedding feast for their king. Among the invited guests were their neighbors the centaurs. But the centaurs behaved monstrously. They brought no gifts. They ate too much, and they drank too much. And worst of all, they tried to steal the bride away by force. In fact, they soon tried to carry off all the Lapith women to their woodland home. Fighting broke out between the Lapiths and the centaurs, and people never again offered centaurs their hospitality.

There was, however, one centaur who was wise and civilized. He was so wise and so civilized that he became the teacher of the god Apollo. His name was Chiron.

SOURCE NOTE

The monsters whose stories I have chosen appear again and again in both Greek and Latin literature. References to them in *The Oxford Classical Dictionary*, *The Metamorphoses of Ovid* (A. E. Watt translation), *The Oxford Companion to Classical Literature*, and *The Greek Myths* by Robert Graves were particularly helpful.

Greek art aspired to an ideal of perfect beauty and often avoided depicting the monstrous or grotesque. Therefore, while I found the art from ancient Greece very beautiful, it was often less useful as reference for my illustrations than those forms that appeared in my own imagination after reading descriptions of these remarkable monsters. I hope children who look at my pictures will agree that this is the way such creatures may well have looked.

PRONUNCIATION GUIDE

These pronunciations are based upon Classical Greek, not Modern or New Testament Greek.
In pronouncing the vowels, the English short vowel sound should be used except for the following:

aa = long a (date)   **ee** = long e (evil)

y = long i (side)   **oh** = long o (hope)   **you** = long u (use)

In each word, the accented syllable is underlined.

Apollo—**a pol loh**
Argos—**ha gos**
Ariadne—**air ee odd ne**
Athene—**a thee nee**
Centaurs—**cen taurs**
Charybdis—**ca rib dis**
Chiron—**kee ron**
Circe—**ker ke**
Crete—**kree te**
Cyclopes—**cy clo paace**
Cyclops—**cy clops**
Daedalus—**dy de lus**
Deino—**dy noh**
Dionysus—**di oh ny sus**
Echidna—**hee chyd na**
Empusae—**hem poo sy**
Enyo—**en yoh**
Gorgon—**gor gohn**

Graiai—**gry y**
Hecate—**hee ka te**
Hera—**he ra**
Heracles—**her a clees**
Hermes—**her mees**
Hydra—**hy dra**
Io—**hy oh**
Iolaus—**y oh laa us**
Ithaca—**ith a ca**
Lapiths—**lap eeths**
Medusa—**mee du sa**
Minotaur—**min oh tar**
Naxos—**nax os**
Odysseus—**oh dees se us**
Pegasus—**peg a sus**
Pemphredo—**pem free doh**
Perseus—**per see us**
Polyphemus—**poh lee fee mus**

Poseidon—**poh sy don**
Scylla—**skil la**
Theseus—**thee see us**
Typhon—**ty fohn**
Zeus—in Greek this would be **zaa os**, but it has become an English word pronounced **zooss**

References:
The Oxford Dictionary of Modern Greek, J.T. Pring, ed. Oxford: Clarendon Press, 1982.

An Intermediate Greek-English Lexicon (Founded upon the Seventh Edition of Lyddell and Scott's Greek-English Lexicon). Oxford: Clarendon Press, 1989.

Thanks to Father Robert J. Miner for his help with the pronunciation guide.

Line drawings, silk screened in gold ink and hand colored with watercolors, were used for the full-color art. The text type is Kuenstler 480. Copyright © 1996 by Anne Rockwell. All rights reserved. No part of this book may be reproduced or utilized in any form or by any means, electronic or mechanical, including photocopying, recording, or by any information storage and retrieval system, without permission in writing from the Publisher, Greenwillow Books, a division of William Morrow & Company, Inc., 1350 Avenue of the Americas, New York, NY 10019.   Printed in Singapore by Tien Wah Press   First Edition   10 9 8 7 6 5 4 3 2 1

Library of Congress Cataloging-in-Publication Data
Rockwell, Anne F.   The one-eyed giant and other monsters from the Greek myths / by Anne Rockwell.   p.   cm. Includes bibliographical references. Summary: Relates ten Greek myths featuring an assortment of fantastic creatures.   ISBN 0-688-13809-8 (trade).   ISBN 0-688-13810-1 (lib. bdg.)   1. Monsters—Juvenile literature.   2. Mythology, Greek—Juvenile literature.   [1. Mythology, Greek.]   I. Title.   BL795.M65R63 1996   398.2′093801—dc20   95-12326   CIP   AC